ROSS RICHIE
chief executive officer

MARK WAID
editor-in-chief

ADAM FORTIER
vice president,
publishing

CHIP MOSHER
marketing director

MATT GAGNON
managing editor

JENNY CHRISTOPHER
sales director

FIRST EDITION: MARCH 2010

10 9 8 7 6 5 4 3 2 1
FOR INFORMATION REGARDING THE CPSIA ON THIS PRINTED MATERIAL
CALL: 203-595-3636 AND PROVIDE REFERENCE # EAST – 65771

WRITER:
Jesse Blaze Snider

ART:
Nathan Watson
(CHAPTER 1-4)

INKS: Nathan Watson, Mike DeCarlo, Juan Castro
(CHAPTER 4)

COVER:
MICHAEL CAVALLARO

SPECIAL EDITION COVER:
Nathan Watson

COLORS:
Mickey Clausen
(CHAPTER 1-4)

COLORS:
Eric Cobain
(CHAPTER 4)

LETTERER:
Marshall Dillon
(CHAPTER 1)

DESIGNER:
Erika Terriquez

Deron Bennett
(CHAPTERS 2-4)

EDITOR:
Aaron Sparrow

THE RETURN OF BUZZ LIGHTYEAR

SPECIAL THANKS:
Jesse Post, Lauren Kressel,
Elena Garbo, Lisa Kelley,
and Kelly Bonbright

CHAPTER 1

ANDY, HOW MANY TIMES HAVE I TOLD YOU NOT TO RUN DOWN THE STAIRS?!

SORRY, MOM.

WHAT'S A *"GIFT RECEIPT"*? AND WHAT DOES SHE MEAN *"RETURN IT AND GET SOMETHING NEW?"* YOU CAN DO THAT?!

YEAH, BUZZ...YOU CAN.

THAT JUST SEEMS... *WRONG.*

IT'S LIKE THE POOR TOY NEVER EVEN HAD A CHANCE...

TRUST ME BUZZ...IT'S FOR THE BEST.

"FOR THE BEST?" I THOUGHT YOU'D BE ON MY SIDE.

I *AM* ON YOUR SIDE.

OBVIOUSLY *NOT,* WOODY.

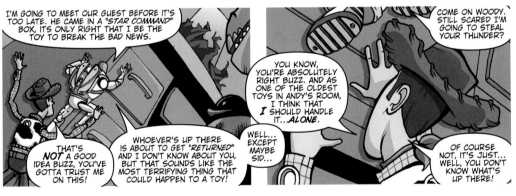

I'M GOING TO MEET OUR GUEST BEFORE IT'S TOO LATE. HE CAME IN A *"STAR COMMAND"* BOX, IT'S ONLY RIGHT THAT I BE THE TOY TO BREAK THE BAD NEWS.

THAT'S *NOT* A GOOD IDEA BUZZ, YOU'VE GOTTA TRUST ME ON THIS!

WHOEVER'S UP THERE IS ABOUT TO GET *"RETURNED"* AND I DON'T KNOW ABOUT YOU, BUT THAT SOUNDS LIKE THE MOST TERRIFYING THING THAT COULD HAPPEN TO A TOY!

WELL... EXCEPT MAYBE SID...

COME ON WOODY. STILL SCARED I'M GOING TO STEAL YOUR THUNDER?

YOU KNOW, YOU'RE ABSOLUTELY RIGHT BUZZ. AND AS ONE OF THE OLDEST TOYS IN ANDY'S ROOM, I THINK THAT *I* SHOULD HANDLE IT...*ALONE.*

OF COURSE NOT, IT'S JUST... WELL, YOU DON'T KNOW WHAT'S UP THERE!

YOU'RE RIGHT. THAT'S WHY I'M GOING UP THERE TO FIND OUT!

OH...

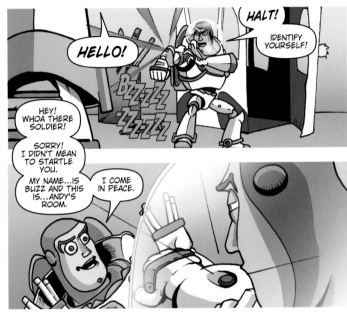

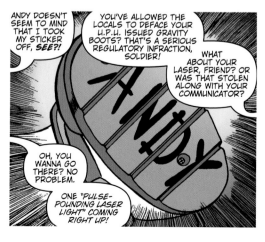

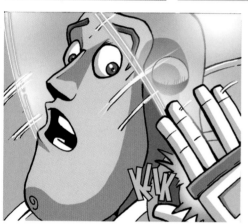

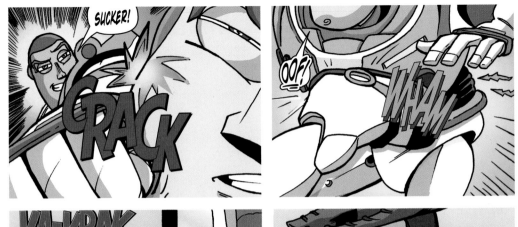

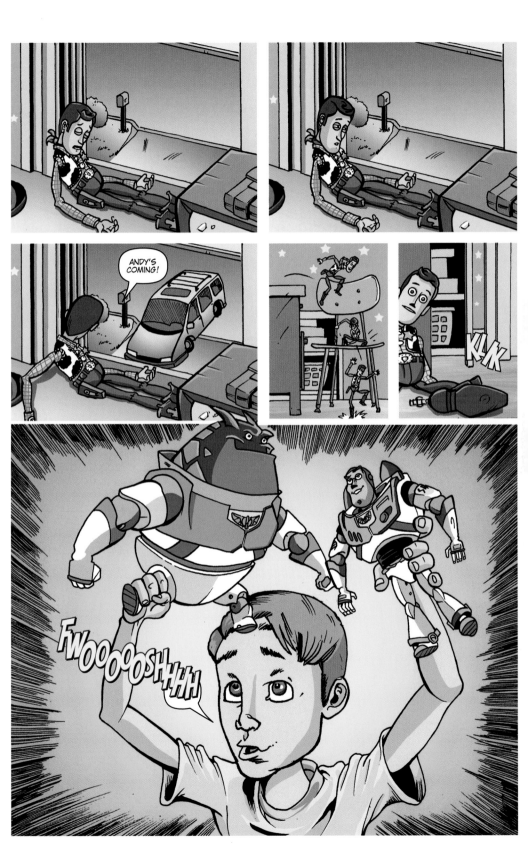

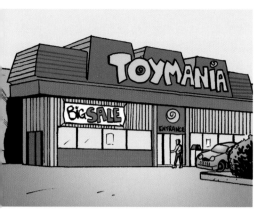

CHAPTER 2

PSST... COMMANDER LIGHTYEAR! COME HERE!

IS THAT YOU, WOODY?

YEAH, IT'S ME. I'VE CALLED AN EMERGENCY PLAYROOM MEETING, SO HURRY UP!

COME ON BOOSTER, WE DON'T WANT TO BE LATE.

RIGHT AWAY, SIR! SORRY!

HELLO? WHERE ARE YOU GUYS?!

WE'RE UNDER THE BED!

IN THE DARK? HOW CAN YOU SEE?

WE HAVE... SPECIAL...NIGHT VISION GOGGLES! DON'T YOU?

OF...COURSE WE DO! NIGHT VISION GOGGLES ARE STANDARD EQUIPMENT FOR ALL STAR COMMAND PERSONNEL.

I DIDN'T GET NIGHT VISION GOGGLES.

ER...? OF COURSE NOT. I MEANT THAT THEY'RE STANDARD EQUIPMENT FOR ALL ELITE STAR COMMAND PERSONNEL.

CAN I HOLD YOUR HAND? I'M AFRAID OF THE DARK.

THAT'S WHY YOU'RE NOT A MEMBER OF THE ELITE.

AT EASE, EVERYONE. I'D LIKE TO INTRODUCE YOU TO OUR NEW RECRUIT BOO--

THUD! CRASH! SMACK!

AAH!

UM, YOU SEE, *YOUR COMMANDER WAS SENT HERE AS AN...AMBASSADOR* FROM STAR COMMAND, BUT WE ALREADY *HAD* AN AMBASSADOR FROM STAR COMMAND. OUR AMBASSADOR WAS TRANSFERRED BACK BY MISTAKE...SO *NOW...WE* HAVE TO TAKE YOUR COMMANDER BACK TO THE *SPACE STATION,* SO WE CAN GET OUR AMBASSADOR BACK!

UNDERSTAND?

COMPLETELY.

THOSE MIND WORMS *REALLY* GOT AHOLD OF YOU.

GAH!!! YOU KNOW WHAT?! YOU'RE RIGHT! I *HAVE* BEEN POSSESSED BY A ZAMBONIAN MIND WORM! IN FACT, WE *ALL* WERE! AND IF YOU DON'T TAKE US BACK TO THE TOY STORE RIGHT NOW...

SPACE STATION.

...TAKE US BACK TO THE SPACE STATION *RIGHT NOW...* REX IS GOING TO *EAT* YOU!

BUT WOODY...I'M A *VEGETARIAN!*

ⁿSIGHⁿ I KNOW *YOU* ARE, BUT YOUR MIND WORM...*ISN'T!*

OHHH... RIIIGHT.

MMMMM... I...*LOVE...MEAT!!!*

DELICIOUS... EXOTIC...NEW KINDS OF... ALIEN...UH, MEAT?!

I'LL DO ANYTHING YOU WANT! JUST KEEP HIM AWAY FROM ME!

GOOD BOY. ALL RIGHT, TOYS AND GIRLS--LET'S *DO THIS!*

SO, WHAT'S THE PLAN WOODY?

SARGE AND HIS MEN ARE ALREADY DOWNSTAIRS GETTING THE KEYS TO ANDY'S MOM'S CAR. REX...HAMM... SLINKY...POTATO...AND BOOSTER, YOU'RE WITH ME.

BO, YOU'RE IN CHARGE OF THE PLAYROOM UNTIL WE GET BACK.

YOU GOT IT, WOODY.

WHEEZY, IF ANYTHING GOES WRONG, YOU'RE OUR DIVERSION.

UH-OH... I KNOW WHAT *THAT* MEANS...

ROCKY, PICK UP "COMMANDER LIGHTYEAR" HERE...AND WELCOME TO THE "A" TEAM!

WHAT?!

HOLD ON HERE, WOODY! ROCKY?! I HEARD A RUMOR THAT A COMBAT CARL ONCE GOT 'IM IN A KUNG-FU GRIP AND *ROCKY* RIPPED HIS ARM CLEAN OFF!

IT'S *NOT A RUMOR.*

SEE?!

WELL THEN, SLINK... I'D SUGGEST YOU DON'T USE ANY OF YOUR ACTION FEATURES AGAINST HIM.

THAT'S NOT FUNNY, WOODY! THIS IS SERIOUS!!!

LOOK, YOU'RE RIGHT, SLINK. ROCKY CAN BE A BIT... *UNPREDICTABLE.* BUT THE FACT IS THAT WITHOUT BUZZ, WE'RE DOWN A MAN, AND HIS SPECIAL... HOW SHALL I SAY... *TALENTS* MIGHT COME IN HANDY.

MOMENTS LATER...

ALL RIGHT, THE **FRONT DOOR** WAS ONE THING, BUT THE **CAR DOOR** WAS GOIN' TOO FAR!

GIRLY TOY.

YOU BET I AM, ROCKY! IF I GET A **KINK** IN MY SLINK, IT AIN'T EVER COMIN' OUT!!!

DO **YOU** KNOW HOW TO **FIX** A **BROKEN** SLINKY?

NO! OF COURSE NOT! NO ONE DOES! A SLINKY **BREAKS...** AND THEY JUST THROW IT OUT AND BUY A NEW ONE! WELL, THAT AIN'T HAPPENIN' TO **ME!** NO-SIR-REE-BOB, WE'RE JUST GONNA HAVE TO FIGURE OUT ANOTHER WAY TO OPEN DOORS FROM NOW ON!

GIRLY TOY.

YOU KNOW, I LIKED YOU BETTER WHEN YOU DIDN'T TALK.

MIKE? WHAT ARE YOU DOIN' OUT HERE IN THE CAR?

ANDY LEFT ME HERE AFTER HIS FRIEND'S KARAOKE PARTY. WHY IS BUZZ ALL TIED UP? WHAT'S GOING ON?

THAT'S NOT BUZZ! Y'SEE, BUZZ KNOCKED BUZZ OUT AND GOT BUZZ RETURNED TO THE TOY STORE, SO WE'RE TAKING BUZZ BACK SO WE CAN RESCUE BUZZ!

FORGET I ASKED.

HEY WOODY, NOT THAT **THIS** ISN'T ENTERTAINING, BUT ARE YOU PLANNING ON, I DON'T KNOW, **DRIVING** US SOMEWHERE ANYTIME SOON?

YEAH, WE'RE BURNING MOONLIGHT HERE!

MY CAR...?

WHO'S IN MY CAR?!

KRSSH!

MY GPS UNIT!

WHAT IS THIS? *GREMLINS* OR SOMETHING?!

VROOOOM!

GOOD WORK, GANG! SORRY ABOUT GETTING US *PULLED OVER.*

THAT'S OKAY, WOODY. I'M SURE LOTS OF PEOPLE GET PULLED OVER FOR DRIVING *TOO SLOW.*

YEAH, THEY'RE CALLED "*OLD LADIES.*"

GOOD THING I PACKED MY DRIVING GLASSES. SO, WHICH WAY WOODY?

I DON'T THINK WE'LL HAVE ANY PROBLEM FINDING OUR OLD FRIEND BUZZ NOW THAT WE HAVE OUR NEW FRIEND...*GPS!*

YOUR DESTINATION, TOY MANIA, IS POINT FOUR MILES WEST AND ON THE RIGHT SIDE OF THE ROAD.

AW, THANKS FOR ALL YOUR HELP.

NEVRLST

MY PLEASURE, WOODY! I HOPE YOU FIND YOUR FRIEND.

WELL, IF WE DO, WE'LL HAVE *YOU* TO THANK, LITTLE LADY.

WILL YOU PLEASE STOP FLIRTING WITH THE GPS UNIT? YOU REALIZE IT'S JUST A SILVER SQUARE WITH DIGITAL LIPS?

I THINK IT'S THAT *VOICE.* HOT, HUH?

YEAH, "*HOT*" AS IN *STOLEN!* YOU DO KNOW YOU CAN SWITCH THE VOICE TO *MALE.*

THAT'S NOT FUNNY, POTATO.

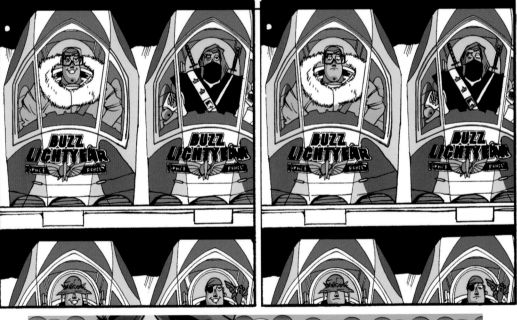

CHAPTER 3

WHO DID I THINK I WAS KIDDING, ANYWAY?

WHAT WOULD ANDY WANT WITH A TOY THAT DOESN'T EVEN *WORK* ANYMORE?

I GUESS *I'D* HAVE RETURNED ME *TOO*.

"TO INFINITY AND BEYOND!!!"

APPARENTLY I'M NOT THE *ONLY* ONE WHO'S MALFUNCTIONING...

SO WE'VE GOT "ARCTIC BUZZ" HERE TONIGHT. I SEE YOU GUYS CAME PREPARED FOR A *COLD* RECEPTION. RIGHT?

OH, NEVER MIND. IT MAY BE COLD IN SPACE, BUT UNDER YOUR HELMET IT'S *ABSOLUTE ZERO!*

WHAT A HOCKEY PUCK!

LOOK EVERYONE-- IT'S "NINJA BUZZ".

WHY AREN'T YOU AN EMPTY PACKAGE? NOW *THAT* WOULD BE NINJA!

THAT'S ABOUT ALL THERE IS TO SAY ABOUT *THIS* NUMB-CHUCK!

HEY, WHO LET *"SLEEPY TIME BUZZ"* OUT OF HIS PACKAGE?

TO NAPTIME *AND* BEYOND!

EASY, BUDDY. SOMEBODY HIT THE SNOOZE BUTTON!

YOU KNOW, I SAW THE COMMERCIAL THAT FEATURED YOU. NOW THAT WAS ENOUGH TO PUT *ANYONE* TO SLEEP!

JUST KIDDING. NICE *SLIPPERS.*

AND WHO ARE YOU LOVELY LADIES SUPPOSED TO BE?

I'LL HAVE YOU KNOW THAT WE'RE "DISGUISE BUZZ!"

DISGUISED AS WHAT, TWISTED SISTER?!

OH, FOR CRYING OUT LOUD, YOU SPACE TOYS HAVE NO SENSE OF HUMOR!

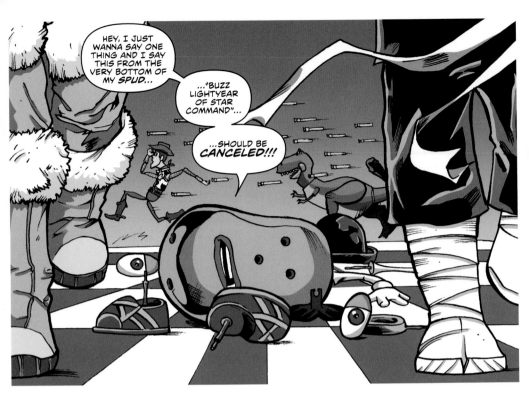

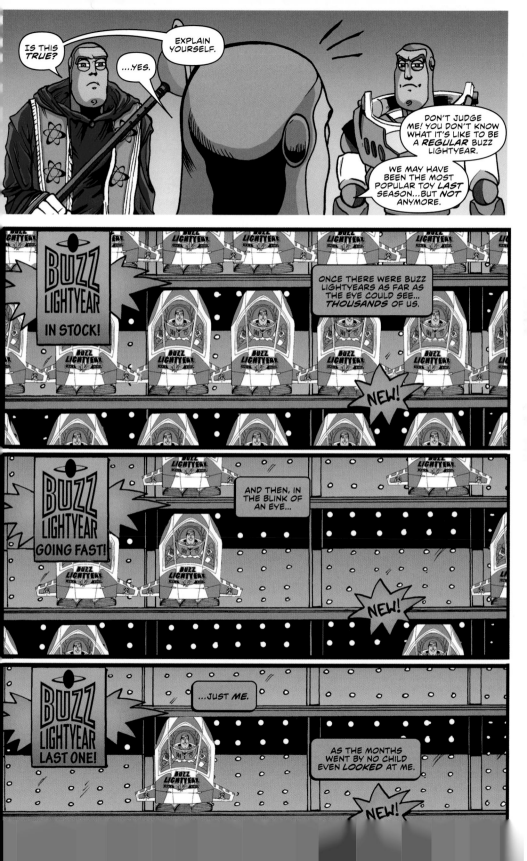

PASSING BY THE PLAIN OLD BUZZ LIGHTYEAR...

...FOR "BATH TIME BUZZ" OR "ARCTIC BUZZ" OR "JUNGLE ATTACK BUZZ."

FINALLY, WHEN I'D LOST ALL HOPE, A PRETTY YOUNG WOMAN PICKED ME UP, SMILED AT ME AND BOUGHT ME FOR HER NEPHEW'S BIRTHDAY.

I WAS SO EXCITED-- I *SWORE* THAT I WOULD MAKE THAT KID *HAPPIER* THAN ANY TOY HE *EVER* GOT!

BUT HE ALREADY *HAD* A BUZZ LIGHTYEAR...

...AND *I* WAS *RETURNED* TO THE STORE...

...FOR THE *FIRST* TIME...

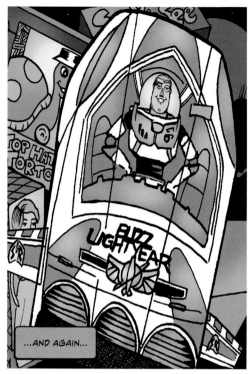

TOYS LIKE ME ARE DESTINED FOR "EBAY" AND A LIFETIME ON A DISPLAY SHELF OR WORSE...IN STORAGE.

WE'LL NEVER KNOW WHAT IT'S LIKE TO BE PLAYED WITH...

...TO BE TRULY LOVED.

EVERY MORNING I ARISE BEFORE OPENING TO HIDE FROM COLLECTORS, THEN SIT ON THE SHELF IN THE AFTERNOON HOPING TO BE SEEN AND PURCHASED BY A CHILD...

...BUT WHAT CHILD WANTS A GLORIFIED POLITICIAN ACTION FIGURE?

THIS RANGER JUST WANTS WHAT ANY OF US WANT. TO ENJOY OUR TIME AS A CHILD'S BELOVED TOY.

...AND SO I PROPOSE A CONTEST.

A RACE AROUND THE WORLD!

HE MEANS THE STORE, RIGHT?

I SURE HOPE SO.

THE WINNER GETS ANDY...AND THE GREATEST PRIZE OF ALL...

...LOVE.

DONE.

CHAPTER 4

I HAD THE **BEST** VIEW...AND *I* SAY *I* WON!

NO WAY! SALLY *MUST* HAVE WON. HE WAS *TACKLED* ACROSS THE *FINISH LINE!*

EH, THAT'S NOT NECESSARILY TRUE, WOODY. THOUGH HE *DID* TACKLE BUZZ, IT'S STILL POSSIBLE THAT HIS FACE, HANDS OR ARMS CROSSED THE LINE *FIRST.*

HEY, WHOSE SIDE ARE YOU ON ANYWAY?!

LISTEN, WOODY, I JUST WENT THROUGH A NEAR DEATH EXPERI-ENCE! I'M A NEW SPUD, AND I NEED TO HOLD MYSELF TO A HIGHER STANDARD OF *TRUTH* AND *JUSTICE!*

I ADMIRE YOUR HONESTY, SOLDIER!

THANKS, SARGE.

ACTUALLY, ALL THEY DID WAS REASSEMBLE YOU WITH YOUR OLD PARTS.

REALLY...?

WELL IN *THAT* CASE, THE WINNER WAS SALLY! I'D STAKE MY EYES ON IT!

YEAH, AND THOSE ARE HIS *BEST* EYES!

HOORAY FOR SALLY!

SALLY BEAT 'IM ALL RIGHT, FAIR AND SQUARE!

THE BEST TOY WON!

WILL EVERYONE *PLEASE* STOP CALLING ME "SALLY"?!

SORRY BUZZ... MY FAULT.

DON'T YOU HAVE SOME SORT OF *FINISH LINE CAMERA,* IN CASE OF SOMETHING LIKE *THIS?*

NOW THAT YOU MENTION IT...

...WE DO HAVE A PICTURE OF THE FINISH.

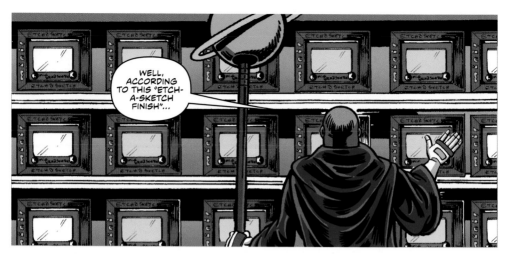

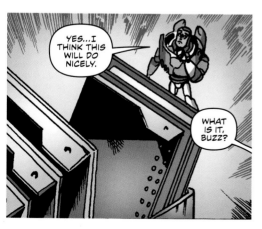

MEANWHILE...

HMM?

OH, IT'S YOU. YOU CAN SAVE YOUR LECTURE...I ALREADY KNOW WHAT I DID WAS WRONG.

THAT'S NOT WHY I'M HERE.

I CAN'T SAY I APPROVE OF WHAT YOU DID, SON...BUT I *UNDERSTAND* IT.

THERE'S NO GREATER FEELING FOR A TOY THAN TO BE LOVED BY A CHILD. IT'S WHAT WE ALL DREAM OF. WHAT WE'RE *MADE FOR.*

IT'S JUST...I FEEL LIKE I'M ONE RETURN AWAY FROM THE CLEARANCE AISLE. I WAS SO DESPERATE, I WAS WILLING TO TAKE THAT LOVE AWAY FROM ANOTHER TOY.

MAYBE I DESERVE TO BE IN THE BARGAIN BIN. I'VE DISGRACED STAR COMMAND, I'VE DISGRACED ALL OF YOU, AND I'VE DISGRACED MYSELF.

THAT'S THE GREAT THING ABOUT REMORSE, SON...

...IT MEANS IT'S *NOT TOO LATE.*

EASY, SPACE RANGER. I COME IN PEACE.

...REALLY.

I THOUGHT YOUR LASER WAS DEAD.

YEAH, WELL...SOMEONE *RETURNED* SOME BATTERIES.

LISTEN...I JUST WANTED TO SAY, I'M SORRY.

THERE'S NO EXCUSE FOR MY ACTIONS. I HAD NO RIGHT TO TRY AND TAKE ANDY FROM YOU. HE'S A GREAT KID, AND HE DESERVES A GREAT TOY...

...YOU.

NO HARD FEELINGS?

WELL...

...A SPACE RANGER NEVER HOLDS A GRUDGE! APOLOGY ACCEPTED!

COME ON BUZZ, LET'S GO HOME.

SLINKY, WATCH YOUR BACKSIDE!

UH-OH...

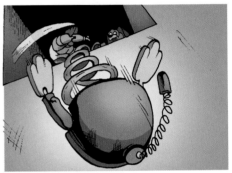

UNGHF!

HE SACRIFICED HIMSELF TO SAVE YOU, BUZZ! OH, THE *HUMANITY!*

A MOMENT OF SILENCE, MEN...

WAIT... LOOK!

5 BY 5, SPACE RANGER! NOW STOP WORRYING ABOUT ME...GET BACK TO YOUR CAR AND BE HOME WHEN ANDY WAKES UP!

GOODBYE! AND... THANKS.

UNGH...

HE'S *ALIVE!*

THANK GOODNESS!

ARE YOU ALL RIGHT DOWN THERE?

MOMENTS LATER...

WELL, THERE THEY GO. DID YOU MAKE AMENDS?

I DID...AND YOU KNOW, I FEEL A LOT BETTER!

OH!

WHAT IS IT?

I...THINK YOU SHOULD HAVE A LOOK.

WH-WHAT...?!

NO, NO, NO!

NO ONE WILL *EVER* WANT *ME* NOW.

LATER THAT MORNING...

DING-DONG!

ANDY, CAN YOU GET THE DOOR?!

...OKAY.

DING-DONG!

YOU WERE RIGHT, BUZZ! BEING A TOY IS THE BEST! ALL THE EXCITEMENT OF STAR COMMAND WITHOUT ANY *REAL* DANGER! I'M GONNA LOVE IT HERE!

JUST BE CAREFUL, BOOSTER! I SAW ANDY'S SISTER LOOKING YOU OVER EARLIER!

GLAD TO HEAR IT, BOOSTER.

I STILL REMEMBER THE TIME SHE CARRIED ME OFF TO HER ROOM...IT TOOK A WEEK FOR ANDY TO NOTICE I WAS MISSING!

AND EVEN LONGER TO DRAIN ALL THE DROOL OUT OF MY COIN SLOT!

IT WAS ONE TIME, HAMM. DON'T TAKE IT TO HEART. YOU AND I BOTH KNOW THAT ANDY LOVES Y--

ANDY, WHO'S AT THE DOOR?!

IT'S THE *POLICE!*

MA'AM, WE'D LIKE TO ASK YOU A FEW QUESTIONS ABOUT YOUR WHEREABOUTS LAST NIGHT?

....HIDE.

THE NEVER-ENDING TOY STORY...

COVER GALLERY

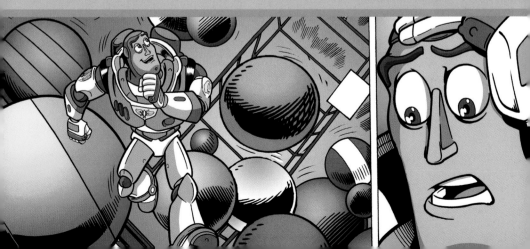

COVER 0A: MICHAEL CAVALLARO

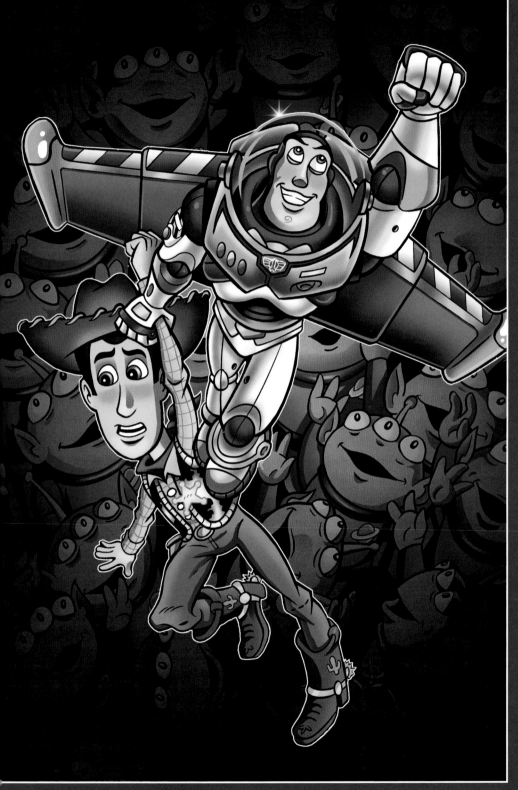

COVER 0B: BRENT SCHOONOVER

COVER 1A: NATHAN WATSON
COLORS: VERONICA GANDINI

COVER 1B: NATHAN WATSON
COLORS: VERONICA GANDINI

COVER 2A: NATHAN WATSON
COLORS: MICKEY CLAUSEN

COVER 2B: NATHAN WATSON
COLORS: VERONICA GANDINI

BUZZ 'SALLY' LIGHTYEAR CHAMPION **VS.** BUZZ 'NEW BUZZ' LIGHTYEAR CHALLENGER

'THE BOOM IN ANDY'S ROOM!'
DIRECT FROM RINGSIDE **THIS MONTH!**

★ ★ ★ ★ ★ ★ ★ ★ ★

COVER 3A: NATHAN WATSON
COLORS: MICKEY CLAUSEN

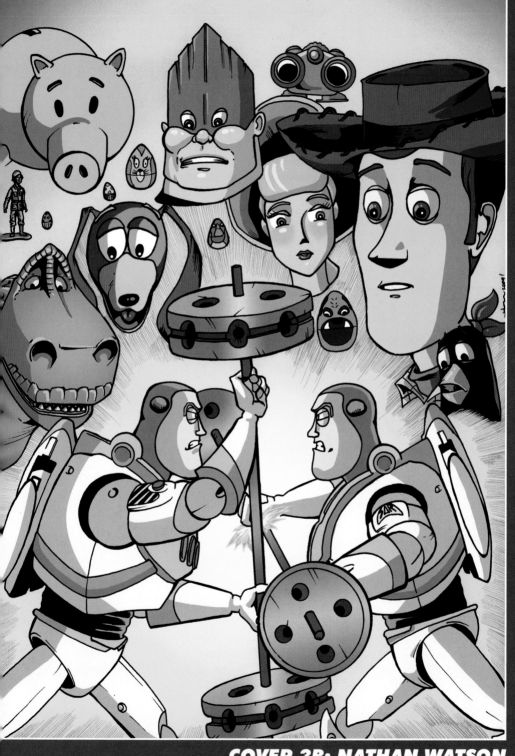

COVER 3B: NATHAN WATSON
COLORS: MICKEY CLAUSEN

MEET THE MUPPETS

This hilarious trade collects the first four issues of THE MUPPET SHOW, written and drawn by the incomparable Roger Langridge! Packed full of madcap skits and gags, The Muppet Show trade is certain to please old and new fans alike!

THE TREASURE OF PEG-LEG WILSON

Scooter discovers old documents which reveal that a cache of treasure is hidden somewhere within the theater...and when Rizzo the Rat overhears this, the news spreads like wildfire! Can Kermit keep everyone from tearing the theater apart?

ON THE ROAD

With the theatre destroyed after the search for the treasure of Peg-Leg Wilson, the Muppets take their act on the road... but with two very familiar hecklers in every town, will the show be a hit, or will our Muppet minstrels be run out of town in tar and feathers? Also: Fozzie and Rizzo have plans for a big budget PIGS IN SPACE motion picture, but is Hollywood prepared?

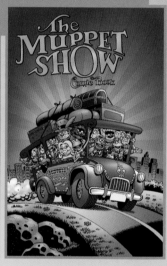

CARS: THE ROOKIE

See how Lightning McQueen became a Piston Cup sensation in this pulse-pounding collection! CARS: THE ROOKIE reveals McQueen's scrappy origins as a local short track racer who dreams of the big time...and recklessly plows his way through the competition to get there! Along the way, he meets Mack, who help McQueen catch his lucky break.

CARS: RADIATOR SPRINGS

From writer Alan J. Porter, this collection of CARS stories is perfect for the whole family! After his return to Radiator Springs, LIGHTNING MCQUEEN is hanging out with his friends at Flo's V8 Café when he realizes that everyone knows his story...but he doesn't know anyone else's! McQueen wants to know how his friends ended up in Radiator Springs...and more importantly why they decided to stay!

WALL-E: RECHARGE

Wall-E is not yet the hardworking robot we know and love. Instead, he lets the few remaining other robots take care of most of the trash compacting while he collects interesting junk. But when the other robots start breaking down, Wall-E must learn to adjust his priorities... or else Earth is doomed!

WALL E: RECHARGE
SC $9.99 ISBN 9781608865123
HC $24.99 ISBN 9781608865543

MUPPET ROBIN HOOD

The Muppets tell the Robin Hood legend for laughs, and it's the reader who will be merry! Robin Hood (Kermit the Frog) joins with the Merry Men, Sherwood Forest's infamous gang of misfit outlaws, to take on the stuffy Sheriff of Muppetham (Sam the Eagle)!

MUPPET PETER PAN

When Peter Pan (Kermit) whisks Wendy (Janice) and her brothers to the magical realm of Neveswamp, the adventure begins! With Captain Hook (Gonzo) out for revenge for the loss of his hand, Wendy and her brothers may find themselves in a situation where even the magic of Piggytink (Miss Piggy) can't save them!

MUPPET ROBIN HOOD
SC $9.99 ISBN 9781934506790
HC $24.99 ISBN 9781608865260

MUPPET PETER PAN
SC $9.99 ISBN 9781608865079
HC $24.99 ISBN 9781608865314

FINDING NEMO: REEF RESCUE

Nemo, Dory and Marlin have become local heroes, and are recruited to embark on an all-new adventure in this exciting collection! Their reef is mysteriously dying and no one knows why!

MONSTERS, INC.: LAUGH FACTORY

Someone is stealing comedy props from the other employees, making it difficult for them to harvest the laughter they need to power Monstropolis... and all evidence points to Sulley's best friend Mike Wazowski!

FINDING NEMO: REEF RESCUE
SC $9.99 ISBN 9781934506882
HC $24.99 ISBN 9781608865246

MONSTERS, INC.: LAUGH FACTORY
SC $9.99 ISBN 9781608865086
HC $24.99 ISBN 9781608865338

DISNEY'S HERO SQUAD: ULTRAHEROES

It's the year 2734 and the only one standing in the way of earth's utter destruction is...Mickey Mouse?! Join the four-colored fun as Mickey Mouse, Goofy, Donald Duck take to the skies to save the world.

DISNEY'S HERO SQUAD: ULTRAHEROES
SC $9.99 ISBN 9781608865437
HC $24.99 ISBN 9781608865529

WIZARDS OF MICKEY: MOUSE MAGIC

Your favorite Disney characters star in this magical fantasy epic! Student of the great wizard Grandalf, Mickey Mouse hails from the humble village of Miceland. Allying himself with Donald Duck (who has a pet dragon named Fafnir) and team mate Goofy, Mickey quests to find a magical crown that will give him mastery over all spells!

WIZARDS OF MICKEY: MOUSE MAGIC
SC $9.99 ISBN 9781608865413
HC $24.99 ISBN 9781608865505

DONALD DUCK AND FRIENDS: DOUBLE DUCK

Donald Duck as a secret agent? Villainous fiends beware as the world of super sleuthing and espionage will never be the same! This is Donald Duck like you've never seen him!

DONALD DUCK AND FRIENDS: DOUBLE DUCK
SC $9.99 ISBN 9781608865451
HC $24.99 ISBN 9781608865512

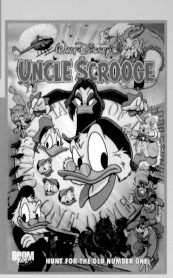

UNCLE SCROOGE: THE HUNT FOR OLD NUMBER ONE

Join Donald Duck's favorite penny pinching Uncle Scrooge as he, along with Donald himself and Huey, Dewey and Louie embark on a globe spanning trek to recover treasure and save Scrooge's "number one dime" from the treacherous grasp of Magica De Spell.

UNCLE SCROOGE: THE HUNT FOR THE OLD NUMBER ONE
SC $9.99 ISBN 9781608865536
HC $24.99 ISBN 9781608865536

THE LIFE AND TIMES OF SCROOGE MCDUCK VOL. 1

BOOM Kids! proudly collects the first half of THE LIFE AND TIMES OF SCROOGE MCDUCK in a gorgeous hardcover collection — featuring smyth sewn binding, a gold-on-gold foil-stamped case wrap, and a bookmark ribbon! These stories, written and drawn by legendary cartoonist Don Rosa, chronicle Scrooge McDuck's fascinating life. See how Scrooge earned his 'Number One Dime' and began to build his fortune!

THE LIFE AND TIMES OF SCROOGE MCDUCK VOL. 2

BOOM! Kids proudly presents volume two of THE LIFE AND TIMES OF SCROOGE MCDUCK in a gorgeous hardcover collection in a beautiful, deluxe package featuring smyth sewn binding and a foil-stamped case wrap! These stories, written and drawn by legendary cartoonist Don Rosa, chronicle Scrooge McDuck's fascinating life.

THE LIFE & TIMES OF SCROOGE MCDUCK VOLUME 1 HC
HC $24.99 ISBN 9781608865383

THE LIFE & TIMES OF SCROOGE MCDUCK VOLUME 2 HC
HC $24.99 ISBN 9781608865420

MICKEY MOUSE CLASSICS VOL. 1

See Mickey Mouse as he was meant to be seen! Solving mysteries, fighting off pirates, and just generally saving the day! These classic stories comprise a "Greatest Hits" series for the mouse, including a story produced by seminal Disney creator Carl Barks!

DONALD DUCK CLASSICS: QUACK UP

Whether it's finding gold, journeying in the Klondike, or fighting ghosts Donald will always have help with Huey, Dewey, Louie, his much more prepared nephews, by his side! Carl Barks brought Donald to prominence, and it's only fair to start off the series with some of his most influential stories!

MICKEY MOUSE CLASSICS: MOUSE MAYHEM
HC $24.99 ISBN 9781608865444

DONALD DUCK CLASSICS: QUACK UP HC
HC $24.99 ISBN 9781608865406

WALT DISNEY'S VALENTINE'S CLASSICS

Love is in the air for Mickey Mouse, Donald Duck and the rest of the gang. But will Cupid's arrows cause happiness or heartache? Find out in this collection of classic stories featuring all your most beloved characters from the magical world of Walt Disney! Featuring work by Carl Barks , Floyd Gottfredson, Daan Jippes, Romano Scarpa and Al Taliaferro.

WALT DISNEY'S CHRISTMAS CLASSICS

BOOM! Kids has raided the Disney publishing archives and searched every nook and cranny to find the best and the greatest stories from Disney's vast comic book publishing history for this "best of" compilation.

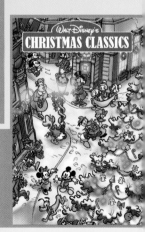

WALT DISNEY'S VALENTINES CLASSICS VOL 1 HC
HC $24.99 ISBN 9781608865499

WALT DISNEY'S CHRISTMAS CLASSICS VOL 1 HC
HC $24.99 ISBN 9781608865482